Ghost Hands

A Story Inspired by Patagonia's Cave of the Hands

T. A. Barron

illustrated by William Low

Philomel Books
An Imprint of Penguin Group (USA) Inc.

Dedicated to the people who painted those hands long ago.   —TAB

To Jennifer, with special thanks to Tim for helping out.   —WL

Dear Reader,

Do you love to travel? I surely do. There is so much to discover in our world!

When I visited South America's Patagonia region, I learned about an especially remarkable place in Argentina. It's called Cueva de las Manos—Cave of the Hands.

The rock walls of this cave are literally *covered* with paintings of hands. Archaeologists have counted a total of 890 separate hands—and, inexplicably, one left foot! The oldest hand paintings are over 9,000 years old. Yet these images—made by blowing paint over people's hands—are still clear and colorful today. The cave has sheltered them all this time from rain, sun and wind.

These hands are the artistic legacy of the Tehuelche tribe, Patagonia's native people. They roamed this region for millennia before Europeans, led by Ferdinand Magellan, arrived in 1520. Just as the Tehuelche wove baskets from the grasses, they wove stories from the threads of their lives—stories about the moon and sun, infants and elders, and the ever-hungry puma they called Goln. They often returned to this cave, a sacred place. But just why they painted all those hands—and that lone foot—remains a mystery.

Sadly, there are no Tehuelche people left to tell us. They were massacred, poisoned and driven away by settlers who wanted the land for sheep farming. The last survivor of these original Patagonians died in 1960. But in Cueva de las Manos, they are not quite gone forever.

The hands in this wondrous cave seem almost alive—waving to us across centuries of time. I would love to meet those artists, to shake their living hands. And I would also love to ask them one question:

Why in the world did you paint that foot?

—T. A. Barron

My people tell many stories—sometimes with our words, sometimes with our hands. Even our names tell stories. Mine is Auki—little hunter.

I had watched my father leave to hunt the bounding guanacos every summer, and dreamed of joining him. For when the calafate berries start to swell, so does the heart of a hunter.

"Let me come with you!" I begged. But always my father told me to wait another year.

So I practiced running like the wind. I practiced hurling a spear and throwing a rawhide rope. I even practiced being patient—but that was something I just could not do.

This summer, I stood as straight as a spear and asked again.

My father frowned. "No, my son. To hunt you must be strong. And brave—brave enough to face the puma. For the puma, too, is a hunter who stalks the guanaco herd. He would kill one of them—or one of us."

The very next day, I left before dawn. If only I could catch sight of the puma and follow him back to his hidden den, I would prove myself worthy of the hunt. Worthy of my name!

But could I really find him? I didn't know. But I could try. By the thunder of Karut, I would try!

Swift and silent I ran through the grasslands, searching for the best spot to wait and watch. It could be anywhere—except in the nearby canyon, a place of great danger. Not just because of its steep, crumbling cliffs, but also because of what those cliffs hid—a secret cave. So secret it was visited only by elders. And also, I'd heard, by ghosts.

I climbed a grassy slope, right to the edge of the canyon. At the top, I could see very far. But no one could see me. The perfect place for a hunter to hide!

Dawn came, stepping across the sky. A hawk made spirals far above me, sunlight shining through her wings. But I saw no sign of the puma.

All day I waited. My skin felt hot, my mouth dry, my legs cramped. I heard the wail of a tero bird, always a warning of evil. But still I waited, trying to be patient.

Then, at the edge of the grass, something moved. Just the wind? Stiffly, I rose to see better.

Puma!

The beast snarled fiercely. I jumped back—and fell down into the canyon like a sack of stones. Helpless, I rolled, slid, bounced and finally slammed onto a ledge.

The world spun. My head ached—but not so much as my foot. Wedged between the rocks, it was badly twisted. Painfully, I pulled free. I tried to stand on the ledge, but my foot screamed. Hobbling over to a boulder, I looked around anxiously. *Where is the puma?*

My foot throbbed, swelling like a waterskin in a stream. I knew I must get back to my family before the puma found me!

Climbing back up would be slow—too slow. My only other choice was to crawl down to the floor of this haunted canyon.

Above me, pebbles clattered down the slope. The puma? I hopped to the edge, then started crawling down the cliffs.

At last, I reached the bottom. Scraped and bruised, I crawled to the canyon stream, a cold white finger that chilled whatever it touched. Just what my foot needed. I thrust it into the water, felt the cold—then gasped.

A cave! Only paces away, it was huge—but somehow not as dark as smaller caves I'd seen. *The secret cave?*

Even in the shadows, its walls glinted with colors. Bright, vibrant colors. Crystals? Jewels?

Despite my aching foot, I crawled closer. Suddenly I realized what they were.

Hands! Everywhere on the smooth rock, even deep in the cave, strange hands waved at me.

Ghost hands! My heart galloped like a fleeing herd.

Just then someone stepped out of the cave. Hunched, with long legs and large ears, he looked more like a hare than a man. He glared at me and said, "Go away, boy!"

"Are you—are you ... a ghost?" I asked.

"Go back to your family."

He stooped to pick up a pair of stones, one bloodred, the other purple. By the mouth of the cave sat more stones. And wooden bowls, full of colored powders and oily pigments.

All at once I understood. "Those aren't ghost hands! You painted them!"

The old man studied his stones with care. "Some of them."

"But why?" The hands still seemed to wave at me.

"Because I am Pajar, painter of our people."

"But why do you paint only hands?"

His eyes narrowed. "You ask too much, boy." He threw the purple stone at my head. "Now go!"

I limped away. But I kept glancing back at the strange old man and his cave. Why would anyone paint a cave of hands? Above me, a tero bird wailed. My foot ached more with every step. Some hunter I was!

Suddenly, I heard a shout.

The old man! Spinning around, I stumbled back to the cave.

Abruptly, I stopped. The puma! Snarling at the old man.

Pajar stood frozen. No way to escape!

I ran toward him, roaring and waving my arms. But I tripped on one of the paint bowls. Green powder sprayed everywhere.

I fell over, legs kicking—just as the puma pounced. My wounded foot smashed into his head, so hard I screamed in pain.

I don't remember seeing the puma run away. I only remember bouncing on Pajar's back as he carried me home.

And I also remember vividly the summer day, weeks later, when the old man came back for me.

Into the canyon he led me, all the way to his cave. My foot still felt tender, and I walked with a limp, but I didn't mind. The whole way, I burned to ask him about those hands. But I waited. For I had learned a little about patience.

As soon as we reached the cave, he spoke. "When you first came here, Auki, you asked a question. Why hands? For many thousand summers, that secret has been known only by elders. And now . . . by you."

Gently, he placed his hand over a painted one.

"These hands threw spears, carried children, found healing herbs, and pointed to the stars. They protected our people, and also our traditions. So that is why this cave holds only hands."

He studied me for a moment. "But today that will change."

"How?" I asked, puzzled.

He took a slow drink from his flask. Then he picked up a bowl of blue pigment, stirred it with a wooden blowpipe, and smiled.

"Today," he declared, "I will paint someone very brave, so brave he saved my life. But Auki, I will not paint your hand."

My people tell many stories—even one about a boy who became a hunter and a painter. Sometimes they tell those stories with words, sometimes with hands.

And once in many thousand summers . . . with a foot.

PHILOMEL BOOKS

A division of Penguin Young Readers Group. Published by The Penguin Group.
Penguin Group (USA) Inc., 375 Hudson Street, New York, NY 10014, U.S.A.
Penguin Group (Canada), 90 Eglinton Avenue East, Suite 700, Toronto, Ontario M4P 2Y3, Canada (a division of Pearson Penguin Canada Inc.).
Penguin Books Ltd, 80 Strand, London WC2R 0RL, England.
Penguin Ireland, 25 St. Stephen's Green, Dublin 2, Ireland (a division of Penguin Books Ltd).
Penguin Group (Australia), 250 Camberwell Road, Camberwell, Victoria 3124, Australia (a division of Pearson Australia Group Pty Ltd).
Penguin Books India Pvt Ltd, 11 Community Centre, Panchsheel Park, New Delhi—110 017, India.
Penguin Group (NZ), 67 Apollo Drive, Rosedale, North Shore 0632, New Zealand (a division of Pearson New Zealand Ltd).
Penguin Books (South Africa) (Pty) Ltd, 24 Sturdee Avenue, Rosebank, Johannesburg 2196, South Africa.
Penguin Books Ltd, Registered Offices: 80 Strand, London WC2R 0RL, England.

Design by Semadar Megged.   The illustrations were rendered on the computer using Adobe Photoshop.
The text is set in 14-point Thesis TheSerif.

Library of Congress Cataloging-in-Publication Data
Barron, T. A.
Ghost hands : a story inspired by Patagonia's Cave of the Hands / T. A. Barron ; illustrated by William Low.—1st ed.   p. cm.
Summary: Auki, a young member of the Tehuelche tribe in Patagonia, wants to prove himself as a hunter but when he sets out on his own to face the puma, he stumbles upon a sacred cave and its guardian.
[1. Cave paintings—Fiction. 2. Courage—Fiction. 3. Tehuelche Indians—Fiction. 4. Indians of South America—Argentina—Fiction. 5. Patagonia (Argentina and Chile)—History—Fiction.] I. Low, William, ill. II. Title. PZ7.B27567Gho 2011 [E]—dc22 2010010648

ISBN 978-0-399-25083-5
1 3 5 7 9 10 8 6 4 2